Highlights Puzzle Readers

LEVEL 2
LET'S READ, READ, READ

Kit and Kaboodle

TAKE THE TRAIN

By Michelle Portice
Art by Mitch Mortimer

HIGHLIGHTS PRESS
Honesdale, Pennsylvania

Stories + Puzzles = Reading Success!

Dear Parents,

Highlights Puzzle Readers are an innovative approach to learning to read that combines puzzles and stories to build motivated, confident readers.

Developed in collaboration with reading experts, the stories and puzzles are seamlessly integrated so that readers are encouraged to read the story, solve the puzzles, and then read the story again. This helps increase vocabulary and reading fluency and creates a satisfying reading experience for any kind of learner. In addition, solving Hidden Pictures puzzles fosters important reading and learning skills such as:

- shape and letter recognition
- letter-sound relationships
- visual discrimination
- logic
- flexible thinking
- sequencing

With high-interest stories, humorous characters, and trademark puzzles, Highlights Puzzle Readers offer a winning combination for inspiring young learners to love reading.

This
is Kit.

This is
Kaboodle.

They love to **travel**.
You can help them on
each **adventure**.

As you read the story,
find the objects in each
Hidden Pictures
puzzle.

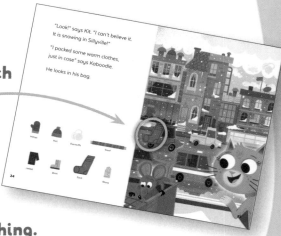

Then check the
Packing List on
pages 30–31 to make
sure you found everything.

Happy reading!

ROADTRIP   AQUARIUM   BOATING

HAVE
FUN

BASEBALL!

OCTOBER

1	2	3	4	5	6
8	9	10	11	12	13
15	16	17			
23	24	25			28
30	31				

OUR
TRIP!

TRAVEL
RIDE THE
ROADS

2 3

Kit and Kaboodle want to go to Sillyville.

"How will we get there?" asks Kaboodle.

"I will give you two hints," says Kit.
"We are not taking a car or a plane.
You will hear *choo-choo* sounds.
Can you guess how we'll get there?"

"We are taking a train trip!"
says Kaboodle.

"Yes," says Kit.
"We are taking a train trip to Sillyville!"

"Let's pack," says Kaboodle.

Kit finds a small suitcase.
"I hope this is not too big," she says.

Kaboodle finds a big suitcase.
"I hope this is not too small," he says.

Kit packs a few things.
"I'm ready!" she says.

Kaboodle packs a few things.
Then he packs more things.

"There is so much to pack.
It will take hours!" he says.

Toothbrush   Comb   Camera   Alarm Clock

Toothpaste   Book   Hair Dryer   Umbrella

The next day, Kit and Kaboodle
go to the train station.

"I hope I packed enough,"
says Kaboodle.

"I hope I did not pack too much,"
says Kit.

"I'm hungry," says Kit.
"Let's get a snack."

"I packed a few snacks,"
says Kaboodle.

He looks in his bag.

Cinnamon Bun

Banana

Muffin

Apple

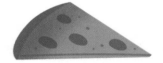

Slice of Pizza

Hot Dog

Slice of Watermelon

Doughnut

TRAIN →

PETE'S
EATS

YUM
SN

ICE
CREAM

"All aboard!" says the conductor.

The train starts moving.

Kit and Kaboodle look out the window.

"Look at all the colorful trees.
I see a tree with yellow leaves,"
says Kaboodle.

"I found it!" says Kit.
"I see a tree with red leaves."

"I found it!" says Kaboodle.

"There is so much to see," says Kit.
"Let's make a picture
to remember our trip."

"I packed a few things
we can use to make a picture,"
says Kaboodle.

He looks in his bag.

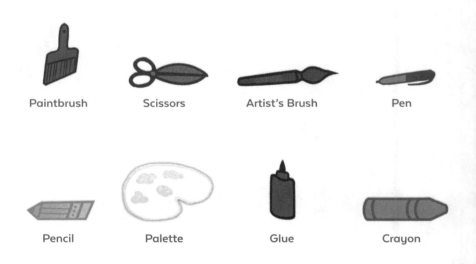

Paintbrush   Scissors   Artist's Brush   Pen

Pencil   Palette   Glue   Crayon

Suddenly, the train goes up.

"We are going up!" says Kit.

"We are going over a mountain!"
says Kaboodle.

"Look at all the mountains!"
says Kit. "How many can we count?"

Clickety-clack. Clickety-clack, goes the train.

"The train makes a fun sound," says Kit. "Let's play to the beat!"

"I packed a few instruments," says Kaboodle.

He looks in his bag.

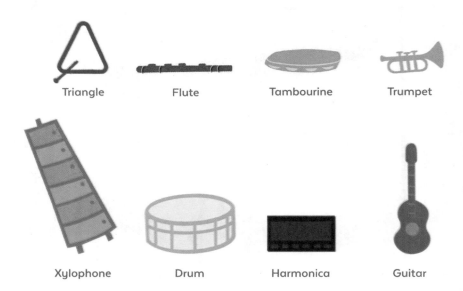

Triangle Flute Tambourine Trumpet

Xylophone Drum Harmonica Guitar

Kit and Kaboodle play
and sing silly songs.

They make some new friends.

Everyone plays and sings
until the conductor calls,
"Next stop, Sillyville!"

"Look!" says Kit. "I can't believe it. It is snowing in Sillyville!"

"I packed some warm clothes, just in case," says Kaboodle.

He looks in his bag.

Mitten   Knitted Hat   Earmuffs   Scarf

Jacket   Boot   Sock   Glove

Kit and Kaboodle get ready
for the cold weather in Sillyville.

The train stops.

They say good-bye to their new friends.

They gather up their things.

"I packed too much," says Kit.

"I did not pack enough," says Kaboodle.

"Hooray! We're here," says Kit.

"What a fun trip!" says Kaboodle.

"We make a good team," says Kit.

"Where should we go
on our next trip?" asks Kaboodle.

Skateboard   Ship   Sailboat   Plane

Canoe   Bicycle   Train   Car

Did you find all the things Kit and

 Alarm Clock

 Apple

 Artist's Brush

 Boot

 Camera

 Canoe

 Crayon

 Doughnut

 Drum

 Glue

 Guitar

 Hair Dryer

 Knitted Hat

 Mitten

 Muffin

 Pencil

 Plane

 Sailboat

 Skateboard

 Slice of Pizza

 Slice of Watermelon

 Toothpaste

 Train

 Triangle

Kaboodle packed for their trip?

Banana

Bicycle

Book

Car

Cinnamon Bun

Comb

Earmuffs

Flute

Glove

Harmonica

Hot Dog

Jacket

Paintbrush

Palette

Pen

Scarf

Scissors

Ship

Sock

Tambourine

Toothbrush

Trumpet

Umbrella

Xylophone

For information about permission to reprint selections from this book,
please contact permissions@highlights.com.

Published by Highlights Press
815 Church Street
Honesdale, Pennsylvania 18431
ISBN (paperback): 978-1-68437-934-7
ISBN (hardcover): 978-1-68437-986-6
ISBN (ebook): 978-1-64472-226-8

Library of Congress Control Number: 2019940916
Printed in Melrose Park, IL, USA
Mfg. 07/2022

First edition
Visit our website at Highlights.com.
10 9 8 7 6 5 4 3 (pb)   10 9 8 7 6 5 4 3 (hc)

This book has been officially leveled by using the F&P Text Level
Gradient™ Leveling System.

For assistance in the preparation of this book, the editors would like
to thank Vanessa Maldonado, MSEd, MS Literacy Ed. K–12, Reading/LA
Consultant Cert., K–5 Literacy Instructional Coach; and Gina Shaw.